D1020230

Real Reads

WUTHERING HEIGHTS

EMILY BRONTË

Retold by Gill Tavner
Illustrated by Vanessa Lubach

an imprint of
WINDMILL BOOKS
New York

Published in 2010 by Windmill Books, LLC
303 Park Avenue South, Suite # 1280, New York, NY 10010-3657

CREDITS:
Author: Emily Brontë
Retold by: Gill Tavner
Illustrator: Vanessa Lubach

Publisher Cataloging In Publication

Tavner, Gill
Wuthering Heights / Emily Brontë ; retold by Gill Tavner ; illustrated by Vanessa Lubach.
p. cm.—(Real reads)
Summary: In this retelling set in nineteenth-century Yorkshire, the passionate attachment between a headstrong young girl and a foundling boy brought up by her father causes disaster for them and many others, even in the next generation.
ISBN 978-1-60754-670-2 (lib.). – ISBN 978-1-60754-671-9 (pbk.)
ISBN 978-1-60754-672-6 (6-pack)
1. Yorkshire (England)—Juvenile fiction [1. Love—Fiction 2. Country life—England—Yorkshire—Fiction 3. Yorkshire (England)—Fiction 4. England—Fiction] I. Brontë, Emily, 1818-1848. Wuthering Heights II. Lubach, Vanessa
III. Title IV. Series
[Fic]—dc22

Printed in the United States of America

CPSIA Compliance Information: Batch #BW10W: For further information contact Windmill Books, New York, New York at 1-866-478-0556.

CONTENTS

THE CHARACTERS

Nelly Dean

Nelly has been a servant at Wuthering Heights for many years. Does she simply observe events, or does she help to shape them?

Heathcliff

Nobody knows where he came from, but Heathcliff's arrival brings trouble. Is he naturally cruel? Is his anger justified? Who will he destroy in his quest for revenge?

Catherine Earnshaw

Can Catherine's wild, free, and passionate spirit ever be tamed? Will her strong character lead to contentment or to tragedy?

Edgar and Isabella Linton

Edgar is wealthy, gentle, and kind. Can he protect those he loves, including his sister Isabella, from Heathcliff's hatred?

Hareton Earnshaw

Hareton is the son of Heathcliff's greatest enemy. Will Heathcliff destroy him too?

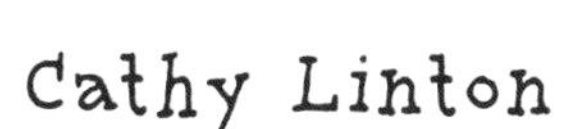

Cathy is Edgar and Catherine's daughter. Can her father protect her from Heathcliff's desire for revenge?

Will Heathcliff's weak son live long enough to fulfill his father's plans for him?

WUTHERING HEIGHTS

Do the souls of the dead roam the earth, yearning and mourning their lost lives and their lost loves? If you spend a little time here with us, on the bleak and lonely moors, you might soon believe so. Our position here at Thrushcross Grange is favorably sheltered, yet nature can still be wild and frightening. Four miles away, at Wuthering Heights, the atmosphere is altogether more violent, and sometimes treacherous.

Wuthering Heights stands alone on an exposed ridge. It is a wind-blasted, fate-blasted house. The country folk fear its mood of horror and darkness, a mood reflected in the lives of those who have loved, hated, suffered, and died within its thick walls. If you care to visit, you will see that the trees have been bent by merciless strong winds, just as the souls of the generations within have been bent by strong passions.

My name is Ellen Dean, but you can call me Nelly. I have served the families at Wuthering Heights and Thrushcross Grange for more than thirty years without seeing any ghosts, but there are folk who tell different stories.

Just over a year ago, a city gentleman, Mr. Lockwood, was renting Thrushcross Grange. I was working here to serve him. Lost on the moors one evening in a violent snowstorm, he was faced with the unwelcome necessity of seeking shelter at Wuthering Heights. The master of the house at the time, Mr. Heathcliff, was a gruff, intense, and tormented man. Heathcliff and I had grown up together, so I knew him as well as anyone; well enough to know that he hated strangers, and was not a willing host.

That stormy evening, poor Mr. Lockwood was savaged by Heathcliff's dogs and cursed by their master. Then he was shown to a dark, mildewed, oak-paneled closet in which, he told me the following day, he spent the most horrifying night of his life.

Alone in his dark room, with only a flickering candle for company, Mr. Lockwood felt strangely drawn toward the window. Outside, the storm was still raging. Placing his candle on the windowsill, he noticed writing carved into the painted wood. He traced with his finger, in all kinds of characters both large and small, the names Catherine Earnshaw, Catherine Heathcliff, and Catherine Linton, each repeated again and again. He retired to his bed, put out his candle, and fell into a restless sleep. His mind and, it seemed, the room, were swarming with Catherines.

Alternately dozing and waking, Mr. Lockwood became aware of a persistent tapping of a branch against the window. In order to silence this relentless teasing, he felt his way to the window. It was locked. Driven by his desperation to sleep, Mr. Lockwood punched out a pane of glass and thrust his arm into the freezing air to grasp the branch. Imagine his horror when, instead of a branch, his fingers closed on a delicate, deathly-cold hand. In his panic he tried to pull his arm back, but the cold hand clung to it. “Let me in, let me in,” sobbed a melancholy voice. “I lost my way on the moor. I have come home.”

Mr. Lockwood could now discern a child’s face, its tears blending with the water running down the window. “Who are you?” he asked, terrified.

"I am Catherine. I have been lost on the moors these twenty years." The voice grew mournful and pleading, "Please, let me in."

Her grasp was strong. Mr. Lockwood, made cruel by terror, pulled the thin wrist against the broken glass until the blood ran. Freed at last from the icy fingers, he piled books against the window. The wailing continued, accompanied by feeble scratchings at the window pane. When the pile of books began to move, Lockwood cried out in a frenzy of fear.

The tortured soul outside fell silent, but Lockwood's scream had woken Heathcliff. Massive, pale, and trembling, he appeared at the closet door. "What is that damned noise? God confound you, Mr. Lockwood."

"I am already confounded, sir. Your house is swarming with ghosts. If that little fiend Catherine had got in at the window..."

"Catherine?" Heathcliff thundered. "Did you say Catherine? How dare you!" Attempting to control his violent emotion, Heathcliff turned toward the window. He seemed to wipe a tear roughly from his eye. “Your childish outcry has ended my sleep. Go to my room. I will stay here.”

Mr. Lockwood obeyed, but was unsure where to go. As he hesitated outside the chamber, he heard Heathcliff wrench open the window and burst into a passion of grief. “Come in, oh my heart’s darling!” he cried in anguish. “Please hear me, Catherine. Come home!”

Mr. Lockwood does not visit us at Thrushcross any more, and Heathcliff died only a month ago. You might think that is the end of Heathcliff's story, but it is neither the end nor the beginning.

Local folks claim that the souls of Catherine and Heathcliff are not at rest, and that they haunt the moors. With passionate natures and a tragic tale such as theirs, perhaps they will never find eternal rest.

I will tell you their tale from the beginning, for I grew up with them both. As a young servant in their house, I saw everything. They told me everything. I played a part in everything.

Catherine was a wild, mischievous child, always singing and laughing. Her father, Mr. Earnshaw, was kind, sensible, and loving toward Catherine and her older brother Hindley. They were a happy family, until the night Heathcliff arrived at Wuthering Heights. I remember it well.

That particular evening, Mr. Earnshaw returned from a business trip to Liverpool. Instead of gifts for his excited children, he brought with him a filthy, ragged, black-haired gypsy boy, about Catherine's age. We all stared.

"He was starving on the streets," explained Mr. Earnshaw tiredly. "I could not leave him to die." The boy stared sullenly, uttering gibberish that none of us could understand. Catherine spit at it. Hindley angered his father by hitting it. I was ordered to wash and clothe it, although I must admit, I was frightened. It looked as if it came from the devil himself.

They called the boy Heathcliff. He was a silent, uncomplaining child, and gave me so little trouble that I gradually softened toward him. I cannot say that I liked him though. He was too closed.

He did not, however, remain closed to Catherine. After a few days of running together over the moors, the two of them became firm friends. Before long the greatest punishment we could invent for Catherine was to be separated from her new companion.

Mr. Earnshaw also grew fond of this uncomplaining boy. Hindley, however, remained cruel. He continued to hurt Heathcliff at any opportunity, enraging his father. Eventually, Mr. Earnshaw sent Hindley away to college. I suppose Hindley must have felt that Heathcliff had pushed him out of his rightful place in the family, which helps to explain his later cruelty.

From the start, Heathcliff never cried or shouted when Hindley hit him. I grew to believe

Heathcliff incapable of resentment or revenge. As you will learn, I was deceived completely.

Over the years, Mr. Earnshaw's strength left him. When he died it broke our hearts. It was a wild October evening, and we were all sitting peacefully by the fireside. Mr. Earnshaw dozed in his usual chair. Catherine, sitting at her father's feet, rested against his knees. Heathcliff was lying on the floor, his head in Catherine's lap. Mr. Earnshaw stroked his daughter's hair while she sang him gently to sleep. "Why can't you always be a good girl, Catherine?" he smiled. Then his fingers dropped from her hair and his head sank on his breast. Looking up at his face, Catherine discovered her loss directly.

"Oh Heathcliff, he's dead." They both let out a heart-breaking cry. I ran to fetch the parson. When I returned I found Catherine and Heathcliff comforting each other with innocent images of Mr. Earnshaw at peace in heaven. Surely nobody has ever pictured heaven as beautifully as they did that night.

Hindley came home for his father's funeral, surprising us all by bringing with him a wife who was even younger than he was. Taking up his position as master of Wuthering Heights, Hindley immediately banished Heathcliff from the family's presence.

"I hate Hindley. He makes poor Heathcliff labor outside like a servant," Catherine complained. "He won't let us eat together or play together. He swears he will reduce Heathcliff to nothing. He won't even let him read books."

At first Heathcliff bore his downfall well. Catherine played with him whenever she could, and secretly supplied him with books. One of their greatest pleasures was to run wild on the moors until darkness fell, growing more reckless each day. They laughed at their punishments, and planned their revenge. I could not know then how firmly the spirit of revenge was settling within Heathcliff's young soul.

Time passed and little changed. Another family, the Lintons, lived here, at Thrushcross Grange. The Lintons made little impact on our daily lives. Their two pale, refined children, Edgar and Isabella, were of no interest at all to the two wild souls of Wuthering Heights. At least, that's what I thought.

One Sunday evening, however, something happened to introduce change, and to introduce the Lintons into our world.

That evening, when I called Heathcliff and Catherine in to supper, they didn't come. Hours passed, and I grew anxious. As darkness fell, Heathcliff returned alone and breathless. "Where is Catherine?" I asked.

"At Thrushcross Grange," he panted. "We wanted to see how those feeble Linton children spend their time. We watched them through a window. Oh, Nelly," his eyes shone, "it was beautiful, all crimson and gold. Catherine and I would have been happy in such a heaven, but those two idiot children were arguing and crying. They're the same age as us, Nelly, but they behave like babies!"

"You shouldn't have gone to the Grange," I chastised him.

"I wish we hadn't, Nelly. Hearing our laughter, Edgar and Isabella bleated like lambs for their parents, 'Oh Mama, oh Papa!' Mr. Linton set the bulldog loose. We ran, but the dog caught Catherine's ankle. 'Run, Heathcliff!' she shouted, but I stayed. I shoved a stone in the brute's throat, but it wouldn't let go."

"Where is Catherine now?" I asked.

"She was hurt. Mrs. Linton came out and recognized her, and Mr. Linton carried her inside."

"Did they invite you in too?" I asked Heathcliff.

"No, Mrs. Linton looked at me with disgust and closed the door on me. But I watched through a window, and could see that they looked after Catherine well. Oh Nelly, her spirit kindled a spark in even their dull eyes. She is so superior to them, to everybody on earth, isn't she, Nelly?"

Poor Heathcliff. Catherine spent five weeks recovering at Thrushcross Grange. For Catherine they were five weeks of fine clothes and flattery; for Heathcliff those five lonely weeks heralded great and unwelcome change.

Catherine came home on a pony, and Hindley lifted her down. "Look at Catherine!" he exclaimed to his wife, Frances. "My savage little sister is now a dignified young lady!" He called to Heathcliff. "Heathcliff, look at Catherine's white silken clothes. Come, shake hands with her. Feel how her hands have grown soft and white. They have not been touched by dirt or sunlight — or by you — for five weeks."

Heathcliff appeared from the shadows. After five weeks of neglect, his thick, uncombed hair was even more filthy than usual. His face and hands bore weeks of dirt. He hung back with either shame or pride, or both.

Laughing, Catherine rushed to him and covered his face with kisses. "Heathcliff, how dark and angry you look!"

Heathcliff scowled. Hindley and his wife laughed cruelly.

Catherine looked down at her dress, brushing off some dried mud that had fallen from Heathcliff. Heathcliff noticed, and his face darkened further. "You did not have to touch me," he sulked. "I like to be dirty. You do too, or at least you used to."

Catherine laughed awkwardly. "Oh Heathcliff, at least shake my hand."

"I will not shake hands or be laughed at," he said quietly.

Catherine looked troubled as Heathcliff returned to the shadows from which he had appeared.

Catherine now spent less time outdoors with Heathcliff. Happy to encourage Catherine's friendship with Edgar, Hindley welcomed the Lintons' increasingly frequent visits. Whenever the Lintons visited, Heathcliff was not allowed in the house. I like to think that I gradually took Catherine's place as Heathcliff's confidante.

One day, when the Lintons were expected, Heathcliff approached me. "Nelly," he began shyly, "can you make me decent? I want to be good today. I should so like to please Catherine."

I led him to a mirror. "First you must smooth away your frown. Cast out the fiends from your eyes and replace them with innocent angels."

"You mean I should wish for Edgar Linton's blue eyes and pale brows?" he replied sadly. "Whatever I do I cannot make Edgar less handsome. I wish I had his fair hair and skin. I wish I had a chance of being as rich as him."

"Oh Heathcliff, Edgar Linton looks like a

doll beside you. You are twice as broad across the shoulders. Where is your spirit?" I found him clean clothes, washed his face, and brushed his hair before leading him again to the mirror. "Now tell me whether you don't think yourself rather handsome," I said admiringly. "I'll tell you, I do."

The Lintons arrived, smothered in cloaks and furs, and were welcomed into the house. Heathcliff stepped forward to greet them, eager to show his new attitude.

Hindley stepped forward briskly and shoved him roughly aside. "Nelly, please lock Heathcliff away until dinner is over. If I see him down here again I shall pull his long hair and make it even longer."

Edgar giggled. "It's quite long enough already. Why, it's like a horse's mane!"

Ashamed and burning with hatred for his rival for Catherine's affection, Heathcliff could not control his violent temper. He seized a bowl of hot apple sauce from the table and threw it into Edgar's face.

Edgar wailed, while Hindley dragged Heathcliff upstairs. I scrubbed Edgar's face clean with more force than was strictly needed.

"Why did you speak to him, Edgar?" complained Catherine, clearly upset. "Now he'll be whipped. I hate it when he is whipped. Why are *you* crying? Nobody is going to whip *you*!"

Later that evening I sneaked some food upstairs to Heathcliff. He was deep in thought. "I'm planning my revenge on Hindley," he said darkly. "I don't care how long I have to wait. I only hope he will not die before I ruin him."

Six months later Hindley's wife gave birth to a son, Hareton. Within a few weeks of giving birth, the poor woman died of tuberculosis. She had always been sickly compared with those of us brought up on the moors. Instead of weeping, Hindley cursed. He turned to drinking and gambling. Instead of devoting himself to looking after Hareton, he instructed me to raise him. He started to treat Heathcliff with a savage ferocity which would have made a fiend out of a saint.

Catherine was now a beautiful fifteen-year-old. In the Lintons' refined company she was graceful and amiable, winning Edgar's heart and soul. In Edgar's absence, however, she was haughty, headstrong, and arrogant. I no longer liked her.

Unable to match the qualities of his rival, Heathcliff lost any self-esteem he had once had. He developed an inward and outward repulsiveness, and a slouching, dirty

appearance. Giving up on his attempts to keep up with Catherine's learning, he told me, "I have no desire to rise when I am forced to sink."

One afternoon, I overheard an argument between Catherine and Heathcliff.

"Why do you prefer those pitiful Lintons to me?" asked Heathcliff sullenly.

"You are dull. You don't say anything interesting."

Heathcliff's reply was quiet. "You never told me before that you disliked my company."

I was drawn away from my eavesdropping by the arrival of Edgar Linton, glowing with love and optimism. Heathcliff stormed from the house. It was not a good time for Edgar to arrive.

"Nelly, go away," said Catherine, ill-humored after her conversation with Heathcliff, "I do not want servants around when I have guests."

Her rudeness made me angry. Welcoming the opportunity to embarrass her in front of Edgar, I refused to move. Catherine checked that Edgar was not looking before she pinched my arm hard enough to hurt.

"Ouch! Miss! That was a nasty trick!" I looked to see Edgar's response.

Catherine was ablaze with a passion she could no longer conceal. She stamped her foot and slapped me across the face.

Edgar's amiable face was pale, his blue eyes wide with disbelief. "Catherine, love!" He held Catherine's shoulders in an attempt to calm her, but instead drew her fury upon himself. The astonished boy felt the sting of Catherine's hand across his own cheek.

We all fell silent.

Quietly, his lip quivering, Edgar walked toward the door. "I must go," he whispered. "I am afraid and ashamed of you."

"No," pleaded Catherine, her eyes glistening with tears. "I will be so miserable if you leave."

With dismay, I saw Edgar soften and hesitate. By the end of the afternoon, I observed that the fight had merely served to break down any barriers that remained between them.

That evening I was busy in the kitchen. Catherine put her head around the door and whispered, "Are you alone, Nelly?"

"Yes," I replied.

"Oh Nelly," Catherine sat down opposite me. "Edgar has asked me to marry him. I'm very unhappy!"

"You are hard to please!" I replied, continuing my chores. I had not forgotten her earlier behavior.

"I have accepted him. Nelly, do you think I was right?"

"Do you love him?"

"Of course. He is handsome and he is rich. I will be the greatest woman in the neighborhood."

"So where is the obstacle?"

"In my soul and in my heart I am convinced I am wrong!"

I looked up.

"Oh Nelly, if I died and went to heaven, I would beg to be sent back to Wuthering Heights. I am no more suited to Edgar than I am to heaven. I am suited only to Heathcliff, but Hindley has brought him so low that it would degrade me to marry him."

I noticed a slight movement behind Catherine. For the first time I became aware of Heathcliff's presence in the shadows. He rose silently from his bench and, unnoticed by Catherine, left the room.

Catherine continued. "Heathcliff will never know how much I love him. He is essential to me. Heathcliff is more myself than I am. Our souls are the same. Nelly, I am Heathcliff."

"Then why marry Edgar?"

"If I marry Heathcliff, we would be poor beggars. If I marry Edgar, I can use Edgar's wealth to free Heathcliff from my brother's power."

"You understand little of the duties of marriage, miss."

I left Catherine deep in thought and continued to prepare dinner. When it was ready, I called Heathcliff in. He did not come.

I searched in vain. Thunder was growling and the dark sky threatened rain. I must admit that I took some pleasure in telling Catherine that Heathcliff had overheard the earlier part of our conversation, and that his disappearance was her fault.

"What did he hear?" she cried, turning pale. "What have I said?" She rushed outside.

That night, while I sat waiting for Heathcliff and Catherine to return, the wind was so strong that it split a great branch from one of the fir trees, which fell across the roof, damaging a chimney. Several hours later, cold, wet, and despairing, Catherine returned alone.

It would be a long time before we saw Heathcliff again.

Three years after Heathcliff's disappearance, Catherine married Edgar and we all moved here to Thrushcross Grange. Ever afraid of upsetting his wife, Edgar loved Catherine cautiously, as a honeysuckle might embrace a thorn. They seemed to be in possession of a fragile but growing happiness, which needed careful nurturing.

It was not to last. Six months later, before their love had developed firm enough roots, trouble arrived. As I came in from the garden

one evening, I heard a voice behind me. "Nelly?"

Turning, I saw a tall young man step from the shadows. The moonlight revealed dark brows and deepset eyes. "Heathcliff?"

"Is Catherine at home?" he asked.

I nodded, too astonished to speak.

"Go and tell her someone wishes to see her."

I hesitated.

"Tell her. Until you do I am in hell."

That evening, with Catherine and Heathcliff absorbed in mutual joy at seeing one another again, poor Edgar struggled to remain polite.

"Tomorrow I will think this was a dream," said Catherine, breathless with delight. She must have been as aware as I was that Heathcliff's athletic stature and strong features made Edgar appear small and child-like by comparison. Heathcliff's dark eyes had gained dignity, but behind them still lurked a fiery ferocity.

"I have fought through three hard years," Heathcliff told Catherine. "I want you to know that I struggled only for you; my gains have been for you alone."

I had a bad feeling that it would have been far better for us all if he had stayed away.

You will be astonished to hear that Hindley invited Heathcliff to stay at Wuthering Heights. I told you earlier that Hindley began gambling after his wife's death. He was now greatly in debt. I think he hoped, over time, to win all Heathcliff's new wealth for himself. It was like a lamb inviting a wolf to dinner.

Edgar could not easily oppose the visits of such a close friend of Catherine's to Thrushcross Grange. Like Hindley, but less willingly, he opened his door to a wolf.

Perhaps we should have foreseen the trouble ahead. Heathcliff was a striking man, and Isabella was an innocent and impressionable young girl. Yet none of us guessed why Isabella grew sickly and irritable until the day I heard her confess her feelings for Heathcliff to Catherine.

To her credit, Catherine was truly concerned for Isabella. I believe it was this concern, rather than jealousy, which led her to warn her sister-in-law, "Do not deceive yourself. Heathcliff's rough exterior conceals no tenderness. He is a fierce, pitiless man. He would marry you for your fortune and then crush you like a sparrow's egg."

When Isabella accused her of jealousy, Catherine grew angry, and when Catherine was angry she became cruel. During one of Heathcliff's visits, Isabella entered the room. Catherine smiled. "Look, Heathcliff, here is somebody that dotes on you even more than I do."

Heathcliff looked towards me.

"No, not Nelly. Isabella."

Isabella, mortified, tried to escape from the room, but Catherine held her.

Heathcliff glanced at them with little interest. “She looks like her brother,” he growled. “If I married her I would want to bruise her face the colors of the rainbow and turn her blue eyes black.”

Struggling free, poor Isabella fled the room in tears.

“She is her brother’s heir, is she not?” said Heathcliff quietly. “Thank you, Catherine, for telling me Isabella’s secret. I will make the most of it.”

I felt that I had to warn Edgar of the danger facing his sister, but perhaps I shouldn’t have interfered. Catherine later said that she could have persuaded Heathcliff to leave Isabella alone, but by then I had told Edgar, who took it upon himself to confront Heathcliff.

A few weeks later Heathcliff visited Thrushcross Grange. A determined Edgar blocked the doorway. "Your presence here is moral poison," he declared.

Heathcliff laughed, "Catherine, this lamb of yours threatens like a bull." He pushed past the trembling Edgar.

Humiliated and furious, Edgar turned and swung his fist at Heathcliff, catching him in the throat. Caught off guard, Heathcliff gasped for breath.

Catherine quickly ushered him to the door. "Leave us, Heathcliff. I will deal with Edgar."

Catherine turned back to Edgar with tears in her eyes. "Your violent jealousy will make me ill," she told him. "You know how dangerous it is to provoke me."

Edgar replied with sorrowful despondency. "Catherine, you will have to choose. Will you give up Heathcliff, or will you give up me?"

Fortunately for Edgar, Catherine did not have to make that choice. Heathcliff found another way to hurt him. The next morning, when I went to wake Isabella, her room was empty. She, not Catherine, had made her choice between the two rivals.

Catherine's intimations of ill health were more real than I had thought. Slowly but surely, her troubled mind succumbed to the power of her passions. "Nelly, I am near my grave," she would groan. "Oh, how I wish I were at Wuthering Heights, a girl again, wild and free!"

Now pregnant with Edgar's child, her body joined her mind in feverish bewilderment. One minute she would be violent with madness, the next a weak child leaning helplessly upon my arm. "Whose face is that?" she would scream, gazing into the mirror. "Nelly, this room is haunted!" Then her terror would turn to stinging hatred. "Nelly," she would hiss at me, "everything is your fault. You are the enemy within." I found it very hard to pity her.

Isabella sent me a letter. "I wish I could visit Catherine and Edgar," she wrote, "but my husband locks the doors. I was a fool. He is not a man, but a devil. I would be less afraid of a tiger than I am of him."

As Catherine weakened, Edgar kept a loyal vigil. When her fever possessed her entirely, he would hold her, weeping.

On one of the rare mornings when Edgar was drawn away on business, there was a loud knock at the door. News of Catherine's decline had reached Wuthering Heights.

"Where is she?" breathed Heathcliff, hot from his hurried journey. "Out of my way, Nelly!"

By the time I arrived, panting, to her room, Heathcliff already had Catherine in his arms. He was covering her face with frantic kisses. "Oh Cathy, my life! How can I bear it?"

Catherine's fevered, confused eyes looked reproachfully at Heathcliff. "How many years do you mean to live after I am gone, Heathcliff? How soon will you forget me?"

"I cannot forget you any more than I can forget myself," groaned Heathcliff. "You will be at peace, but I will be in hell. How can I live with my soul in the grave?"

Catherine raised her arms to hold him. "Oh Heathcliff, I wish us never to be parted."

He pushed her away. "Catherine, you are cruel

and false! Nothing, not even death, would have parted us, but you did it of your own will. Why did you betray your own heart?"

I heard the sound of Edgar's horse below the window, and warned them.

"Catherine," he held her again, "I can forgive the suffering you have caused me, but how can I forgive what you have done to yourself? I must go now, but I will stay outside your window."

That afternoon, with Edgar at her side, Catherine gave birth to a baby girl.

Born two months early, she was tiny and weak. Hours after her birth, her mother died.

When I went downstairs to tell Heathcliff, his eyes were wet, his breast heaving. He already knew. “I cannot live without my soul!” he howled like a savage beast. “Catherine! Do not rest while I am living. Haunt me!”

Catherine was buried in the corner of the churchyard, where the moor climbs in over the tumbledown wall.

Edgar, grieving, retreated from the world. Over time, however, he found comfort in his lovely, lively daughter, whom he named Cathy and in whom he saw something of the love he had lost.

Heathcliff sought comfort in hatred rather than in love. Edgar had caused his childhood separation from Catherine, and then Edgar had caused her death. Edgar’s sister, Isabella, would suffer.

Treated cruelly by Heathcliff, Isabella hated and feared him. When she became pregnant with his child, she knew that she had to escape, both for her own sake and for her child's safety. A year after the death of Catherine and the birth of Cathy, Heathcliff's son was born in London. Isabella called him Linton.

During the passage of the next twelve years, Cathy grew into a beautiful girl with her mother's dark eyes and the Lintons' blonde curls. She brought sunshine back into Edgar's life.

Although I no longer visited Wuthering Heights, I kept up on events there. Hindley died, ruined by gambling and deeply in debt to Heathcliff. Formerly cast in the role of servant, Heathcliff was now the master. I heard from the housekeeper that Hareton, now a strong youth, was kept in ignorance of his rightful position as heir to the Heights. Instead of inheriting his father's property, Hareton was subservient to his father's greatest enemy.

Isabella wrote regularly to Edgar, describing her son as a frail boy who was frequently ill. Seriously ill herself and knowing that she had only a short time to live, she begged Edgar to look after her son after she was gone. Twelve-year-old Linton must never fall into his father's hands.

Cathy, Linton, Hareton—three cousins whose paths would soon cross. Three cousins whose lives would be shaped by Heathcliff's hunger for revenge.

After Isabella's death, Edgar's attempts to keep his nephew safe from Heathcliff soon failed. He was powerless against the boy's father. With sad resignation, he asked me to deliver poor, frail Linton to his fate.

"So you've brought it to me, have you, Nelly?" Heathcliff laughed scornfully. He glared at his trembling son. "It's even weaker than I expected! I am ashamed to call this pale, whining wretch my own. It will barely last until it is eighteen." Heathcliff turned toward the kitchen. "Hareton, come here. Show this thing to its room.'

For the first time in years I saw Hareton, the boy I had nursed. At eighteen years old, he looked strong and handsome, even though he was dressed in a worker's clothes. He was a fine bloom lost in a wilderness of neglected weeds.

"Nelly, don't leave me," cried Linton as Hareton dragged him from the room.

Heathcliff sat down. "Well, Nelly," he said, grimly triumphant, "my son has now risen above Hindley's son. Part of my vengeance is complete."

"What more could you want?"

"I want Linton to marry Edgar's darling daughter. Then my descendants — should my pathetic son live long enough to father children — will be masters of Thrushcross Grange."

Cathy had something of her mother's spirit, but a gentler nature. She delighted to ride her pony around the Grange lands. Just after her sixteenth birthday, she persuaded me, against her father's wishes and against my judgement, to go with her to see Wuthering Heights.

On the way, we encountered Heathcliff. His wicked smile told me immediately that he knew exactly who Cathy was. “Come in and rest,” he offered with false hospitality. “I should like you to meet my son.”

Resisting my attempts to take her straight home, Cathy followed Heathcliff. This misguided visit formed the beginning of a secret friendship between her and Linton. They wrote letters to each other regularly, and Cathy visited Linton whenever she was able. She felt a mixture of sympathy and fondness for her selfish, whining cousin, but she was not in love with him.

Heathcliff was anxious to bring about a marriage between Cathy and Linton before Linton’s declining health failed. It was an important part of his plan for complete revenge. However, to do so against Edgar’s wishes and against the natural wishes of the two cousins involved, he would have to force matters.

The crisis came when Heathcliff refused to allow Cathy to leave after one of her visits. She was a prisoner at Wuthering Heights.

The prisoner wept. "Please let me return to my father. He will be so worried. He is ill. He needs me. This will weaken him."

"Do you think I care?" laughed Heathcliff. "I will let you see your father only as Linton's wife. Marry him, and you will be free to visit your father."

Linton was too terrified of Heathcliff to ever oppose his wishes.

Poor Cathy. Not only was she forced into marriage, but Heathcliff did not keep his word, and refused to allow her to visit her father. Grief, and the shock of these events, proved too much for Edgar, who quickly weakened. He began to yearn to be buried beside his Catherine. Then the day he longed for finally arrived.

A short time after attending her father's

funeral, Cathy nursed her new husband through the final stages of his short, sad life. Although she lived on, all life seemed drained from her. Heathcliff forced his widowed daughter-in-law to move to Wuthering Heights, where her harsh and loveless life made her bitter. Her sunshine faded.

Heathcliff had finally achieved his revenge. Hareton and Cathy, the children of his two enemies, Hindley and Edgar, were in his power. Now he could make them just as miserable as he was.

Thrushcross Grange now being empty, I returned to my former position in the misery and darkness of Wuthering Heights. As the months passed, however, I began to detect unexpected changes in the three inhabitants. Cathy and Hareton were developing an closeness which brought the unfamiliar sound of laughter into the house. I expected Heathcliff to be angered by this, but he seemed to withdraw into himself.

You will remember that Heathcliff had always found me easy to talk to. It should not surprise you, therefore, to learn that one morning he found me in the kitchen. He sat down on the very bench from which he had once heard the words from Catherine which had led to his flight from Wuthering Heights.

"She is always with me, Nelly," he began.

"Who?"

"Catherine. I see her in everything. When I look down at the floor I see her features in the stone. When I raise a hand to strike Hareton or Cathy, I see Catherine in their eyes. Oh, why must they both have her eyes?" His voice was anguished. "She haunts me, Nelly.

She has haunted me since the day she was buried."

I felt an uncomfortable chill. I did not want him to continue, but I was powerless to stop him.

"That night, I walked back to the graveyard. I needed to hold Catherine in my arms again. I began to dig with all my might. When the spade scraped her coffin, I worked to loosen the screws. I was about to open the coffin when I heard something. A sigh. I looked up. Nobody was there.

I started work again, but soon felt the warm breath of another sigh close to my cheek. I knew that Catherine was there. I felt her presence. I could almost see her."

"You should not have disturbed the dead," I shivered.

"I did not disturb her; it is she who has disturbed me for these past eighteen years. Oh Nelly, in death she has tortured me just as she tortured me in life. When I walk on the moors, I feel her presence but I cannot see her. Every night I hear her at my window, but when I open it, she is not there. This torture is killing me."

"You are still strong and hearty," I replied, although my voice faltered. He was trembling, staring straight past me with a strange joy in his eyes.

I followed his gaze, but saw nothing.

"You are right, Nelly, I am strong, but I have to remind myself to breathe. I have to remind my heart to beat. I wish this long fight were over."

"You must not talk like that."

"Listen, Nelly. When the gravedigger was preparing Edgar Linton's grave next to hers, I paid him to open up one side of her coffin — the side facing away from his. Nelly, you must make sure that I am buried on that side, with the side of my own coffin open to her. I long for the day when my body will dissolve with hers; Catherine's remains and mine will be indistinguishable from each other." Heathcliff stood, wiping sweat from his forehead. "I am near my heaven, Nelly. I can almost see her."

The next morning I found Heathcliff lying on the bed in the paneled room, with the window wide open. His lips were smiling, his eyes sharp and fierce. Although he was dead, I could not close those eyes.

I made sure Heathcliff was buried according to his wishes. He is with his Catherine at last. I am sure that their souls have finally found rest. I don't pay much attention when country folks say that, on misty days, they still see Heathcliff and Catherine walking over the moors.

Heathcliff died about a month ago. Hareton and Cathy will be married soon. As owners of both Wuthering Heights and Thrushcross Grange, they will at long last restore light to these dark places.

The weather is gentle today, and we have spent too long indoors. Let us walk over the moor to the churchyard. I will show you the three headstones. They tell their own story.

FOR FURTHER INFORMATION

The Original Work

This *Real Reads* version of *Wuthering Heights* is a retelling of Emily Brontë's magnificent work. If you would like to read the full novel in all its original depth and drama, many complete editions are available, from bargain paperbacks to beautifully bound hardbacks. You will find a copy in your local library or bookstore.

Filling in the Spaces

The loss of so many of Emily Brontë's original words is a sad but necessary part of the shortening process. We have had to make some difficult decisions, omitting subplots and details, some important, some less so, but all interesting. We may also, at times, have taken the liberty of combining two events into one, or of giving a character words or actions that originally belong to another. The points below will fill in some of the gaps, but nothing can beat the original.

- In the original version of *Wuthering Heights,* Mr. Lockwood is the first narrator. Through his diary and through conversations with Nelly, he tells us about his early visits to Wuthering Heights.
- When Nelly takes over telling the story, she is actually telling it to Mr. Lockwood.
- The order of events in the original is a little more complicated than in our version, as Mr. Lockwood meets the adult Cathy and Hareton at the beginning of the story.
- In the oak-paneled room, Mr. Lockwood reads Catherine's diary, which reveals her childhood feelings for Heathcliff.
- Another colorful character, Joseph, plays an important role in the original. He is a strict and sinister servant. He speaks in a colloquial Yorkshire dialect, for example: "T' maister's down i't' fowld. Go round by th'end ot' laith, if ye went to spake to him." For further colorful examples, read the original.

- Grief, drink, and gambling ruin Hindley. He is a violent man.
- We never find out about Heathcliff's past, or how he makes his fortune during the years he is away from Wuthering Heights.
- Catherine tries to dissuade Heathcliff from running away with Isabella, but fails. Heathcliff treats Isabella with great cruelty.
- Early in their relationship, Cathy treats Hareton with disdain. We are led to feel sympathy for Hareton.
- Nelly does not present Linton as a likeable character.
- Heathcliff succeeds in forcing his son's marriage because Edgar is dying. He will not let Cathy visit her father until she marries Linton.
- Heathcliff is cruel to his daughter-in-law, who becomes quite a different person at Wuthering Heights.

Background Information

Emily Brontë was born in Yorkshire in 1818, the fifth of six children. She lost her mother and her two eldest sisters to tuberculosis at an early age. For many years, her father was the curate of the parish church at Haworth in Yorkshire, a county in the north of England. The moorland landscape around Haworth is vividly described in *Wuthering Heights*. The four surviving Brontë children played on the moors, and spent much of their rather isolated lives studying and writing. The three girls continued writing into their adult lives.

Wuthering Heights, published in 1874, is Emily's only novel, while *Jane Eyre* is her sister Charlotte's best-known work. The third sister, Anne, wrote two novels, *The Tenant of Wildfell Hall* and *Agnes Grey*.

The Brontës would have been very aware of historical and political events in their lifetime. Victorian England was in a period of great change, moving from an agricultural economy toward industrial nationhood. This disturbed the old rigid class structure. Part of the tension in *Wuthering*

Heights arises from the fact that Heathcliff's social position is never certain, and he moves between the classes, therefore blurring the boundaries.

Emily Brontë's writing displays the influence of two literary traditions. The first, romanticism, values strong emotions, the wildness of nature, and natural behaviour. Romantic writers often explored the relationship between nature and human emotion, and questioned the need for control and restraint. The second is the gothic tradition, portraying mysterious, dark and brutal characters, and exploring the world of ghosts and spirits.

For Further Reading

Books

- Barnard, Robert. *Emily Brontë*. New York: Oxford University Press, 2000.
- Brontë, Charlotte. *Jane Eyre*. New York: Vintage Books, 2009. (Many editions available, including a *Real Reads* version)

- Dinsdale, Ann. *The Brontës at Haworth*. London: Frances Lincoln Publishers, 2006.
- Kenyon, Karen Smith. *The Bronte Family: Passionate Literary Geniuses*. Minneapolis, MN: Lerner Publishing, 2002.

Web Sites

- To ensure the currency and safety of recommended Internet links, Windmill maintains and updates an online list of sites related to the subject of this book. To access this list of Web sites, please go to www.windmillbooks.com/weblinks and select this book's title.

Films

- *Wuthering Heights*, MGM, 1939. Directed by William Wyler.
- *Wuthering Heights*, Paramount, 1992. Directed by Peter Kosminsky.

- *Wuthering Heights*, ITV, 1999. Directed by David Skynner.

Food for Thought

Here are some things to think about if you are reading *Wuthering Heights* alone, or ideas for discussion if you are reading it with friends.

In retelling *Wuthering Heights* we have tried to recreate, as accurately as possible, Emily Brontë's original plot and characters. We have also tried to imitate aspects of her style. Remember, however, that this is not the original work. Thinking about the points below, therefore, can only help you begin to understand Emily Brontë's craft. To move forward from here, turn to the full-length version of *Wuthering Heights* and lose yourself in her wonderfully descriptive writing.

Critical Thinking Questions

- How do you feel about Nelly? How far do you trust her version of the story?

- Choose an event in the story and tell it through the eyes of one of the characters involved, instead of Nelly's.
- How much sympathy do you feel for Catherine? Why?
- How much sympathy do you feel for Heathcliff as a boy? Why? Does this change as he grows up?
- Do you prefer Edgar or Heathcliff? Why?
- How do you think Nelly feels about Heathcliff?
- What do you notice about Catherine and Heathcliff's relationship with their moorland surroundings?
- Choose two out of Cathy, Hareton and Linton. What are they like? How do you feel about them?
- Do you think the end of Nelly's tale is happy or sad? Why?

Themes

What do you think Emily Brontë is saying about the following themes in *Wuthering Heights*?

- love and passion
- change
- revenge
- social class

Style

Can you find paragraphs containing examples of the following?

- descriptions of scenery and weather
- the use of assonance to help create atmosphere
- the use of short sentences to create suspense
- the use of simile to enhance description

Look closely at how these paragraphs are written. What do you notice? Can you write a paragraph in the same style?

Symbols

We see many symbols in everyday life. Writers frequently use symbols in their work to help the reader's understanding. Consider how the symbols below match the action.

- the moors
- ghosts
- the weather
- eyes